IN TIME FOR THE HIGHWAYMAN

GINA'S TIME TRAVEL AGENCY
BOOK ONE

LORI WHYTE

COPYRIGHT

In Time for the Highwayman
Gina's Time Travel Agency #1
By Lori Whyte

Published by November Snow

Digital edition / 2022
Print edition / 2022 - ISBN 978-1-989764-31-2
Large print edition / 2022 - ISBN 978-1-989764-32-9

Cover by: S.L. Paton

This is a work of fiction. Any resemblance of characters to actual persons, living or dead, is purely coincidental.

AI was not used in the creation of this book or cover.

IN TIME FOR THE HIGHWAYMAN

GINA'S TIME TRAVEL AGENCY #1

All she wants for Christmas is a highwayman...

When Cassy impulsively books a holiday for her Christmas break, she has no idea what will happen, because before now she didn't know magic existed, time travel was possible, and roguish highwaymen were great kissers... (Um, yeah, about that last one... What happens in historic England, stays in historic England, right?)

She hadn't been looking for a happily-ever-after from this holiday, but now all she's expecting is a broken heart when she returns to her own time.

Is it too much to hope that magic will grant her one more wish?

Note to Readers: *Be prepared for a quick fall into romance, a brush with Christmas magic, and a fun jaunt to the early nineteenth century England.*

CHAPTER 1

*Be careful what you wish for
because magic is always listening.
Grandma Lucy's Rules to Magic and Dating*

"Is this a present? Would you like it gift wrapped? I practiced making bows all year, so I'll make it look magical. I promise."

Cassy blinked at the enthusiastic woman across the counter, then looked at the 2000-piece jigsaw puzzle, more chocolate bars than most people ate in a decade, and the obnoxiously tall, teetering stack of romance novels. When she'd selected everything, she'd thought to spoil herself with a little something to look forward to as she struggled to fill the long, long break when her office closed for the holidays in a few days. But seeing everything in one spot made it all look rather... *ugh*... And more to the point, her pity party supplies really didn't need to be gift wrapped. She cleared her throat. "Ah, no, that's okay. Thanks."

The woman's wide and happy smile didn't change as she rang up the sale and handed over the credit card machine.

Her little Christmas tree earrings flashed in time to the Christmas songs on the speakers, which she hummed along to in perfect tune. Both her red sweater and her green pants sparkled like they'd been dipped in fairy dust. If Cassy believed in the magic of the season or any magic at all—she was way too practical for that, despite her Grandma Lucy's insistence that she came from a long line of witches—she'd think the woman was one of Santa's elves in disguise. Because, really, it wasn't natural to be that perky at the end of a dreary, wintery day, on the shortest day of the year even.

Magic is in the air tonight, Grandma Lucy used to say on the winter solstice. *A night for wishes and dreams.*

If only that were true.

But what would she even wish for if she could?

"Wishing you the merriest of Christmases," the cashier said.

Cassy grunted and grabbed the shopping bag.

Stepping out of the shop didn't improve her mood. The sidewalks and roads were full as people hurried to get to holiday parties or finish their Christmas shopping. It didn't help that at barely five o'clock the sky was already dark and had been for a while. She pulled her collar tighter around her neck and ducked her head down to watch for ice on the sidewalk.

Maybe she needed to buy one of those SAD lights or whatever. Sunlight in the evening was a mere memory and she missed it. Just like she missed a lot of things, like having family to spend the holidays with. Before Grandma Lucy, her last relative, had died years ago, the older woman had tried to pass along as many pearls of wisdom as she could. Some of it was pretty specious, though, from the insistence that magic was real to rules for dating a witch—a term that Cassy sincerely hoped her grandmother was using figuratively. Back then, perhaps buoyed by her grandmother's belief that wishes could come true, Cassy had always been convinced she'd have a family of her own to help her celebrate the season. So much for best laid plans.

Blah.

Enough.

It'd been two years since her divorce was finalized and pretty much everyone she knew figured she should be dating again. It made her wonder what was wrong with her that it was taking so long to come to terms with the end of her marriage. It wasn't that she wanted him back. Nope. No way. Not even a little bit. Not after everything that had happened.

No, she wasn't mourning the loss of him at this point, but the loss of all the dreams she'd built around what she'd imagined their life together would be. Not that things had ever felt settled and happy between them, even in the beginning. But she'd thought they shared enough common values, ideals, and ambitions to make it work. She'd been wrong then, and no one had come along since to make her think it would be different the next time.

But maybe her friends were right. Maybe she needed to do something different this year.

The tinkling of small bells floated over the cacophony of people and cars, such a pretty sound over the drone of everyday life. Cassy stopped and looked around. To her right was a small storefront. The air in front of the windows sparkled like one of those Facebook photo filters she'd looked at but never had occasion to use. It had to be a pop-up store, just there for the holidays, but Cassy couldn't remember ever seeing the space before. The bright and welcoming sign said, "Gina's Time Travel Agency: We can take you anywhere, anytime!"

Time travel? She snorted. Right. Some stores had the

weirdest gimmicks to get people through the door. Although holidaying in an ancient Scottish castle for a few weeks would probably be like traveling back in time. She laughed at the idea of her very own holiday movie adventure. A fluttering sensation tickled along the back of her neck at the idea of it.

She stared at the store window. The bulky shopping bag, filled with her enormous bundle of books, hung heavily at her side, like it carried the weight of every bad decision that had led her to this exact moment. Her carefully thought-out plans from the past hadn't worked out, so maybe it was time to try something spontaneous.

It wouldn't hurt to look, right?

The interior of the shop was more like a living room than a travel agency. The walls were covered in expensive looking wood paneling and the floors were polished hardwood. Clustered around a welcoming fire blazing from a massive stone fireplace were four leather club chairs, several side tables, and a long, comfortable looking sofa. A cat and a dog were curled up together on a plush throw rug. Neither of them even lifted their heads to look at her. The travel agent was MIA, as were the brochures and posters that usually cluttered places like this.

"Hello?"

One of the wood panels creaked open and a frazzled looking young woman with wildly curly blonde hair and wire rimmed eyeglasses hurried into the room. Her flowing orange skirt billowed around her knees as she rushed forward. "Oh. Hello. We weren't expecting anyone this afternoon." Then she glanced at the cat and dog. "Were we?"

The cat flicked its tail and cuddled in closer to the dog.

"Do I need an appointment?" Cassy asked. "Sorry, I didn't realize. I was walking by and saw your shop. I thought I would stop in and see what types of holidays you offered. It was a spur of the moment decision."

"Right. Of course. Please come in and make yourself comfortable." The woman gestured toward the seats by the fireplace.

Cassy sat at the end of the sofa, set her package by her feet, and loosened her winter jacket.

The woman brushed her palms over her skirt, then looked at the door from which she'd just come. When nothing happened, she sucked in a deep breath. Her cheeks were flushed with a rosy pink, seeming to betray a nervousness Cassy wasn't sure she understood. "Right. Let's just chat a bit about what you're looking for."

"Is everything okay?"

"Oh, don't mind me. Gina, the owner, is usually the one to help our clients in the beginning. I'm Alice by the way." She held her hand out to shake.

"Cassy." Cassy took Alice's hand. A tingle of *something* zinged up her arm. "Oh, sorry, this time of year is so bad for static, isn't it?"

"Oh, no, that was me. Gina insists we check all our clients before we get too far into any chats. It really isn't enough that you can see the store, you know? Well, of course you know. Still, I want to assure you we take our position in society very seriously. Our services can't be offered to just any old person, can they? The wards on the storefront help a lot, but we still check. We don't want to confuse any mundanes, am I right?" Alice laughed as she settled lightly on the closest chair. She fluffed and adjusted her skirt before turning her attention back to Cassy.

Cassy had no idea what Alice was going on about. Her words made no sense. It was strange, almost as strange as the woman talking to the cat and dog like they could actually respond.

So, all right, then. Alice was a little crazy. Great.

Cassy glanced at the door to the street. She really didn't need to go with this travel agent. Hell, she could just book a holiday for herself online and probably save a bundle. Still, she was here. It didn't hurt to ask, right?

"So, what kind of holiday interests you?"

"I haven't really given it much thought. I'm open to anything really. Do you have any specials on right now?"

"Everything is special," Alice insisted with a wink. "Okay, if you aren't sure, why don't we start with some questions? Many of our clients find it to be helpful."

"Sounds good." Cassy nodded.

Alice pulled open a tiny drawer on the side table closest to her and extracted some papers and a pen, all of which she handed to Cassy. "Let's start with this questionnaire. Oh, you'll need something to write on, won't you?" She turned to dig in the drawer again, this time pulling out a large clipboard. Honestly, Cassy had no idea how all of that had fit in such a small drawer. It must be an optical illusion. "Here you go."

Cassy started to fill out the form. The first part was easy. Name. Address. Phone number. Email address. And then the questions changed: favorite movie, favorite song, favorite book, favorite era, favorite memory, and more. It was more like an online personality quiz. But in for a penny and all that.

It took at least half an hour to complete the paperwork. Throughout it all, a faint whisper spiraled through Cassy. It was almost too quiet to hear anywhere except her heart. It said, *yes, yes, yes.* It said, *finally.* It said, *my friends were right. It's time to think about dating again. Mr. Perfect might not exist, but maybe, just maybe, I could find Mr. Perfect-for-me.* A tiny stirring of hope fluttered through her at the very idea of it.

Her whole body seemed to tingle with anticipation, right down to her fingers holding the pen and the form.

While she was writing out her answers, Alice puttered around the room, adding more logs to the fire, petting the animals, and adjusting the angles of each chair by millimeters. She didn't seem at all bothered with how long Cassy was taking. No one else came through the agency's door. How did a place like this stay in business? Cassy swallowed. How expensive were these holidays?

Anxiety crept up the back of Cassy's neck when she passed the questionnaire back to Alice. Still, she could always say no, right? She wasn't committed to anything just by answering the questions.

Oh, who was she kidding? For some reason, her gut, or instinct maybe, was telling her this was important. Like that little whisper inside her shouldn't be ignored. Like her answers were going to have a big impact on her life. Like this moment would change everything. It was a ridiculous idea, but she couldn't shake the feeling now that she'd identified it. She shoved her worries aside and watched Alice run her fingers over each answer.

"Very good." Alice nodded at something.

"Hmm, interesting. Yes, I could work with that," she said about something else.

Upon arriving at the end of the form, she stared vacantly into the fire for a few minutes. In contrast to the calm and restful room, the air seemed to suddenly buzz with energy.

Cassy cleared her throat.

Alice blinked, shook her head slightly, then smiled brightly at Cassy. "I know just the thing."

When she didn't elaborate, Cassy nodded encouragingly. "And that is?"

"Oh, you want to know ahead of time. Of course, we have

people who do. I just thought you were looking for something different. A present to yourself? A bit of a surprise."

Cassy straightened. She hadn't said anything about that, had she?

"Just a feeling I had," Alice said, rubbing the side of her nose like Santa did in one of those old stories she used to love to read this time of year, back when the holidays didn't equal loneliness. "Anyway, yes. How would you like to stay at an old estate in England for the holidays? I know you mention sunshine and the beach at one point, but this estate will be just a perfect match. Full of late eighteenth to early nineteenth century charm. I've never had the opportunity to visit that era before. It should be exciting."

Visit that era. That was an odd way to describe going on a holiday. Alice clearly took the 'time travel' gimmick seriously. Whatever. Cassy wasn't here to judge their marketing campaign. And, honestly, she was charmed by the idea of what Alice was proposing, so the gimmick was obviously working for her. An estate decked out in historical charm sounded like something out of one of the historical romances Cassy loved. She didn't need a duke or an earl or even a baron like the heroines in her stories did, but a little fling for the holidays might be nice. And if that didn't happen, living in the lap of luxury for a few days didn't sound too shabby either.

"How much?"

Alice named a shockingly reasonable price. There was no reason not to do this.

"Perfect. Sign me up."

Alice clapped her hands. "Wonderful. You are going to have a magical holiday."

CHAPTER 2

When you've eliminated everything else,
it must be magic.
Grandma Lucy's Rules to Magic and Dating

"Merry Christmas to me," Cassy sang to the tune of 'Happy Birthday'. A giddy, weird kind of joy bubbled in her chest at the thought of her holiday plans. Even the last day of work before their Christmas break, which she'd originally been dreading, had been surprisingly relaxed. Then she'd managed to slide through Christmas Eve and the first few hours of Christmas Day with nothing but excitement for her upcoming holiday. With her leaving this morning and returning on New Year's Eve, it'd be a short holiday, but she was determined to make it magical, just like Alice had said.

And now she was just waiting. And waiting. And waiting.

When would her ride to the airport come?

The clock on her microwave said 9:45 am. Okay. So maybe her ride wasn't late. Yet.

Her fingers snapped and unsnapped the buttons on her winter jacket. The weather in England was supposed to be warmish this week, at least warmer than Calgary. Maybe she didn't need her parka. She eyed the closet at her front door. Should she change? But everyone had warned the humidity would make it seem colder.

Had she packed pajamas? Her toothbrush? The zipper on her luggage took approximately three seconds to unzip. She rummaged through her bag for the sixth time so far that morning. Pajamas. Check. Toothbrush. Check. She closed her suitcase again and zipped it up before flopping onto her sofa. Her leg bounced. She had the patience of a cocker spaniel puppy. She had never felt like this before, but some foreign sense of whimsy and excitement had taken hold of her ever since the winter solstice when she'd booked her trip.

Was it reckless to go on a holiday by herself? Shouldn't she be going with a buddy? Alice hadn't even given her the name of the estate so she could pass the information on to someone in case they needed to get in touch with her. Yeah. This was probably the craziest thing she'd ever done. But the tingling sensations she'd always associated with her intuition were quiet and content.

A knock startled her into action. She darted for the door and wrenched it open without looking to see who it was. Alice's cheeks were rosy as she grinned at Cassy from the front step.

"Hi!" Cassy sounded breathless as she smiled at the travel agent. She hadn't expected the same woman who'd booked her holiday to see her off, but the personal touch was certainly going to get them a fantastic review. "Merry Christmas!"

"Merry Christmas, Cassy. Are you ready to go?"

"You bet. I'll just grab my bags."

Alice blinked at her, then blinked at her luggage. "Oh. Um..."

"Is it too much? I wasn't sure what I would be doing, so I kind of packed a little of everything."

"Of course," Alice said as she cleared her throat. "I meant to tell you that the all-inclusive part of the service includes all necessary period appropriate clothing."

"Period appropriate?"

"Eighteenth or nineteenth century, wasn't it?" Alice checked whatever was attached to her clipboard. "Yes. It says so right here. I mean, it isn't a precise practice. I can't choose a specific year, but that is the general era." She squished up her face as she eyed the luggage again. "But, no worries, we'll take it with us and whatever comes through comes through."

Cassy had no idea what that meant but grabbed her bags anyway. She wasn't going to give up everything to live in the past, even for just a few days. She'd seen those reality shows on television when people tried to live like they were in a different era. She'd never seen the appeal. There was a reason why things changed, and some things from the past were meant to stay in the past.

The limo was waiting in front of her house. Her neighbors eyed it curiously from behind their windows. Their suburban neighborhood didn't get a lot of limos. The driver put her luggage in the trunk, then Cassy climbed into the back. Alice followed her inside.

Snow crunched under the tires as they pulled away from the curb. Within a few minutes, they were leaving her neighborhood. She didn't even look back.

"Are you ready for your holiday?" Alice's smile was bright and wide. She looked almost as excited as Cassy.

"Yes. I can't wait," Cassy said.

"Awesome. Let's go," Alice said. She dipped her hand inside her designer handbag. When she brought her hand out again, her fingers appeared coated in glitter. A strange humming vibrated along the back of Cassy's neck. It grew stronger as Alice began to mutter some strange words that didn't sound at all like English. When she finished, Alice winked at her and then blew the glitter right into Cassy's face.

She sneezed violently.

When she opened her eyes again, everything had changed. Like, seriously, every single thing was different.

The limo was some kind of... *carriage*? No, that couldn't be right. But then, under the dim light of a lantern swinging from a hook overhead, she noticed her clothes. Was she wearing a gown and some kind of long coat? She jerked her eyes to Alice. Alice was decked out in a similar way.

"What just happened? Did you drug me?"

Alice's mouth dropped open. "Of course not." Then a blush stained her cheeks. "Was the glitter too much? Everyone has their signature style, and I just thought it'd add a bit of pizzazz. Well, no matter. I'll know better next time."

"What happened to my clothes? And the car? Who undressed me and put me in this?"

Alice's forehead wrinkled. "I don't understand. You were booked on the all-inclusive historical experience. I know people can have a change of heart, but..." The jostling of the carriage slowed a bit. "Oh, dear. Are you cancelling?" Alice sighed. "I will never hear the end of this. Gina said I wasn't ready for a solo trip. Not after the last time. Or was it the time before?"

"You didn't answer my question." Cassy crossed her arms. "What is going on? And don't lie to me."

Alice jolted back like she'd been slapped. "I would never lie."

Cassy looked out the murky window at the darkness beyond. She couldn't see much through the glass, which was streaked and wet with melting snowflakes, so she tried to poke at her intuition to see what it had to say.

Even though it'd been years since she'd used it regularly, the tingling sensation that started at the back of her neck before flowing over her whole body was familiar. Nostalgia came at its heels with bittersweet memories. Her grandmother had always encouraged her to use this part of herself and praised her when she did, calling it magic, which was just a quaint synonym for intuition. After her grandmother's death, Cassy had pushed that side of herself away, hiding from it and the ever-present accompanying grief.

She had tried to access her intuition more in the days since stumbling upon Alice's shop than she had in years. Usually, the practice was a little too loosey-goosey for her practical mind. Of course, when she'd ignored it, she'd ended up married to a man who decided he had no interest in being faithful.

Cassy pushed thoughts of the past away and concentrated on her current situation.

Alice wasn't lying, Cassy's intuition told her that immediately, but something wasn't right. Things around her were misaligned, but she couldn't put her finger on how. Cassy stared out the window and prodded at her intuition to unravel the problem. Or was it that her intuition was telling her to stare out the window? She didn't know, at least not until they passed through a small collection of buildings, all looking like they were from a different era. There were a lot of towns like that in England, right? That's why they filmed historical movies and TV shows here. Of course, accepting that she was currently in England meant she was also accepting she'd been deposited thousands of miles away into a different country in the time it'd taken her to sneeze.

Her heart sped up as she saw a young man hurriedly

sweeping away snow from the front step of one of the buildings. He wore simple trousers and a wool jacket, but they didn't look like anything she'd seen outside of a period movie. And there were horses and carts and lanterns and women in long dresses and...

Cassy swallowed.

If Dorothy could tell she wasn't in Kansas after the tornado, then Cassy could tell she wasn't in Calgary anymore. In fact, she wondered if she was even in the twenty-first century. Or was this some sort of elaborate heritage set? Yes. She liked that idea, but she knew it wasn't the truth. She swallowed hard. Oh, boy, why was it harder to believe it could be a ruse than the real thing?

"What is going on? How did we get here? Where are we?" Then there was the even more troubling question of: *When are we?* She didn't ask that last question. It'd make her sound crazy, right?

"It's magic, silly goose. What did you expect?" Alice laughed nervously, as if she was unnerved by Cassy's questions. At least Cassy wasn't the only one unsettled. "We are Gina's *Time Travel* Agency, aren't we?" Emphasis on *time travel*.

Right, because that didn't sound insane at all.

The horrible thing, though? Cassy suspected Alice was telling the truth. Somehow, her little relaxing getaway had turned into something else entirely.

CHAPTER 3

When all else fails, trust your magic.
Grandma Lucy's Rules to Magic and Dating

Cassy and Alice didn't speak for a long time after that. The world outside the carriage grew darker and Cassy wondered if it was still Christmas Day, just however many years in the past. Alice's words about her luggage and what she'd packed made more sense now. If they really had travelled back in time, her Santa Claus print pajamas wouldn't exactly fit into the era. Would any of her belongings have survived the trip? What would she wear? How would she deal with her hair? Or brush her teeth?

She forced herself to breathe in deeply and exhale slowly.

Okay. Everything would be okay. It was still just a holiday, right? Maybe she could salvage this whole experience by just accepting it and enjoying the novelty of it. The last thing she wanted to do was be returned all alone to her empty little suburban house, watching through the window as families came and went from her neighbors' houses. She hadn't even put up a Christmas tree this year. Whatever happened here had to be better than that, right? It would be an adventure. And Alice seemed to know what to do. She wasn't alarmed by this situation at all.

Maybe it wouldn't be so bad.

"I will admit I am surprised by all of this." Cassy waved her hand through the air, gesturing at the carriage and her clothes and well, everything. "But I don't want to cancel."

Alice let out a long, deep sigh and her shoulders dropped as she relaxed all at once. "Oh, thank goodness. It'll be great, I promise."

"Which leads me to my next question. I'm guessing the trip will be more than just sitting in this carriage."

Alice giggled. "Of course, silly. I don't know why my magic dropped us so far away from the cottage. Usually when we do this, it's only a few minutes before we arrive at our destination." Her forehead wrinkled. "Hmmm... It's strange we haven't arrived yet."

Great. Alice wasn't projecting a great deal of confidence at the moment. That wasn't worrying at all. Not a bit.

"Have you done many of these trips?"

Alice dropped her gaze to the floor of the carriage. "I've been involved with a great number of trips."

"Involved with? But not solely responsible for?"

Alice leaned forward, grabbed Cassy's gloved hand and squeezed it tightly. Her smile was big, and her chin jutted out a little, as if to show her determination. "I promise I will make this an amazing experience for you."

She was enthusiastic enough, that was for sure.

"We will be staying at a small cottage on the edge of the Chattingworth estate. It's a great location, private but still just a short walk down a lane and over a hill to get to the village. The manor house is a short distance away and will be hosting the Winter Ball. Our timing is lucky with that. The largest gatherings usually happen closer to Twelfth Night." Alice clapped her hands excitedly. "And then there are dinner parties and skating excursions and games and, honestly, it will be so much fun."

"You are staying with me the whole time?" Wait, if Alice was here... "Oh, no, did I wreck your holiday plans? I swear I'm over my freak out. I can manage on my own, I'm sure, if you have family you want to spend the holidays with." She had no idea if she could manage on her own, but she wouldn't be responsible for messing up someone else's holidays.

Alice shook her head with a little smile on her face and sat back in her seat. "This is exactly where I wish to be. You'll see. It'll be wonderful. For both of us."

Yeah. That wasn't cryptic at all. What wasn't Alice telling her?

"Well, if that changes—" Cassy started, but then loud noises from outside the carriage interrupted her. What was going on out there?

Then the ominous shout of 'stand and deliver!' rang through the quiet. She sucked in a sharp breath. Her intuition, which she was beginning to suspect she'd be relying on a lot in the coming days, told her this was not a game, a play or an act. Whoever was outside wanted everyone to believe they were a highwayman. But seriously, who said 'stand and deliver' in this day and age? A well-read thug? A robber-historian?

Except this wasn't the twenty-first century, was it? Cassy rubbed her forehead. This was going to take some getting used to.

And, if Cassy and Alice really had been transported to the past, whoever was out there could really be a highwayman, a highwayman who was expecting to walk away with something expensive. Except she didn't own anything a thief would want.

Cassy flinched at every noise and shout and jostle of the carriage.

She'd never been mugged before. What a craptastic way to start her holiday. Across the carriage, Alice's wide eyes darted from window to window. The woman's hands fisted the small bag in her lap. Under her crisp white gloves, her knuckles were probably equally white.

Okay. So, this was probably not one of Alice's scheduled events.

Then the carriage stopped. Cassy could hear voices but couldn't make out the words. Was that the driver? No, 'driver' probably wasn't the right word. Coachman? Whatever. She couldn't think right now. The carriage dude grunted and the whole vehicle rocked, like he was climbing down from wherever he'd been perched to steer this thing.

They waited. One heartbeat. Two heartbeats.

The door swung open to reveal a shadowy winter landscape. Even in the darkness of the winter night, the thin layer of fresh snow sparkled where it lay over the ground. From somewhere beyond the door, horses' hooves stamped on the ground, as if impatient for Cassy to come to terms with all of this.

Snowflakes and a cool breeze gusted inside, decimating the teensy bit of warmth they'd had in the shelter of the carriage. The coat she'd been dressed in wasn't nearly warm enough to ward off the weather. She shivered and reached forward to close the door again, but then a man prowled forward with predatory intent and peered into the carriage. He didn't point his pistol at them, but it was still there in his hand. His grin was full of wicked pleasure as he studied

Cassy and Alice, as if memorizing every detail about them. Cassy tried to do the same to him, but she quickly saw how fruitless her efforts were. The man was concealed from head to foot and every bit of his clothing was black. The only sliver of skin she could see was the bottom half of his face, which his mask didn't cover. So, that's what she concentrated on. Unfortunately, that part of his face was disappointingly normal. There was no scar marring his skin, no gap in his teeth, no dimple in his cheek, and no indent in his chin. Nada. And his eyes were hidden in the shadows behind the holes in his mask, so she couldn't see their color either.

The only curious things were the way his mouth lifted in a wicked smile and how the faint lantern light made his eyes glint like he was being mischievous. It made her want to smile back at him, which was ridiculous given the circumstances. The guy was a highwayman for pity's sake. She shouldn't want to smile at him. Instead, she *should* want to bash him over the head with her handbag or reticule or whatever it was called.

"Good evening, ladies," the man drawled.

Alice cringed against the far side of the carriage.

"You are not who I was expecting." He eyed them thoughtfully for a moment. "No. You are certainly not the elderly Mr. Brewer and the simpering young wife he bought with a promise of jewels and gold." His smile took on a flirtatious quality. "But I am not disappointed."

"We weren't expecting you either," Cassy said. "Perhaps we should all just go our separate ways."

"Ah, an American? How delightful."

She didn't bother correcting his assumption about her origins. Any truth she offered would sound fantastical. She was pretty sure Fort Calgary hadn't even been established yet.

Then the man extended his black gloved hand to her. She eyed it warily. Her intuition, which she was beginning to suspect was faulty from years of neglect, offered no warning about the guy at all. He waggled his fingers at her, beckoning her forward.

Cassy braced her shoulders and stared straight into his eyes. "I'm not going anywhere until you promise you won't hurt us." It was a feeble protest. After all, how would she stop him?

"You shatter me, my lady." His lower lip protruded in an approximation of a pout, but the twinkle in his eyes suggested it was an act. "I would never harm a lady."

Alice flinched at his promise, but Cassy didn't think he was lying. Were gentlemen thieves just fictional or had they actually existed?

The man leaned forward, drawing closer to Cassy. Her heart pounded. Every bit of self-defense knowledge she possessed reminded her that being led away was a bad thing. Her intuition disagreed. For once, she just wished the two halves of her psyche would align and give her an easy answer.

"Come, my lady. We must make haste."

Obviously, delaying wasn't helping matters. So, it looked like she'd be going with her intuition. She crossed her fingers for luck and hoped she wasn't making a huge mistake. Besides, getting him away from Alice, who looked increasingly like she was going to faint or have an aneurysm, would probably be a good thing. Cassy pursed her lips and let him help her out of the carriage. His hand was firm, strong and big enough to envelop her own. Her pulse jumped at the contact and then it felt like a bunch of drunk butterflies went swooping through her stomach. Yeah. Apparently, she had a hand kink. Well, and a body type preference. And a partiality to guys with confidence.

And, yeah, so far this guy, this hoodlum, was ticking all the boxes.

Her feet sank into the snow at the side of the road. It was deep, much deeper than the impractically thin and uninsulated half-boots she wore. Cold brushed against her bare skin just above her ankles. She let loose a string of curses that probably weren't even known by most women in this era and scowled up at the man as he led her to the front of the carriage. If he was surprised by her expletives, he didn't say anything.

"You know, we don't have anything for you," Cassy said, keeping her voice as steady as possible as she squared off against the man. She probably should have pointed that out before she left the shelter of the carriage.

There was movement behind her, but the highwayman held her shoulders, stopping her before she could turn to see what was happening. The weight of his hands on her body felt like an anchor, grounding her in this moment. When was the last time she'd been this close to a man? Probably not since her ex left. She swallowed hard. That was a long time ago. No wonder she was reacting so outrageously to this guy. Under normal circumstances, there was no way she or any other reasonable person would feel attracted to a guy who had attacked her carriage, right?

Except her attraction was embarrassingly real.

She scented a faint hint of alcohol, whiskey maybe, on his breath and a whiff of smoke on his jacket that reminded her of a campfire. Those things shouldn't have been enticing, particularly when she still couldn't see any of his masked face except the sparkle in his dark eyes and his devil-may-care grin. A grin she had a strange urge to trace with her tongue, just to see if he tasted of whiskey too.

"Nothing, hmm?" The man cocked his head to the side.

"Then what is that pretty jeweled comb in your hair? Or the glittering necklace nestled so enticingly at your décolletage?"

Huh. Cassy hadn't known she was wearing any of that. Alice must have given them to her when she'd cast her spell and sent them to this place. Cassy rubbed her forehead. No, she couldn't think about time traveling at the moment. She needed to deal with this man first.

"If I give you these, you'll go away? Leave us? Unharmed?"

"You have my word." The man put his hand over his heart and dipped his head. "You must understand, my lady, it is nothing personal."

What did she care if the man took these things? They weren't hers. She didn't even know what they looked like. And if giving the jewelry to him kept them safe, that was all that mattered.

"Right," Cassy muttered as she yanked the combs out of her hair. She winced as strands of hair came out with them, and her hair fell down to her shoulders.

"Easy, my lady," the man soothed as he brushed his gloved hand over her hair. "Do not harm yourself."

"I'm not a lady, not the way you're thinking." Cassy frowned and thrust the combs at him before tugging off her ridiculous white gloves so she could tackle the necklace next. She'd never be able to work the clasp with gloves on. She pushed the gloves into his hands too. It was either that or tuck them into her cleavage, because she doubted this dress had pockets, and she didn't think drawing his attention back to her so-called *décolletage* would be a good thing.

The man leaned forward until his mouth was close to her ear. "Perhaps you can be *my* lady just the same."

She swore softly and tugged at the clunky jewelry. How was she supposed to do this when he was clearly trying to distract her? Her hands shook as she fumbled with the clasp on the necklace. Her fingers just weren't cooperating.

The man tucked the combs and her gloves into his pockets before pulling off his own gloves. He blew on his hands as if to warm them before lifting them toward her. She bit back a gasp as he bridged the distance between them.

"Hush, now," he murmured. "I just mean to offer assistance."

His fingers danced over her skin, following the trail of gemstones to the back of her neck and the clasp. Her skin tingled with awareness under the light brush of his fingertips. If she leaned into his touch, ever so slightly, who would know? For a highwayman, his hands felt smooth, lacking calluses and the roughness she'd expected. Was he really a gentleman robber? Like Robin Hood? The idea of it made her scoff at her own naivete.

"What are you thinking, my lady?"

As he spoke, his breath fanned over her skin like a caress. He was so very close. All she'd have to do was lift up on her tippy toes and her mouth could brush his. She licked her bottom lip, imagining what his mouth might feel like against hers.

She had imagined having a fling on her holiday, so would it be so very wrong to kiss this stranger? No one would ever know, not even Alice, who was still tucked away in the carriage.

The clasp gave way under the man's fingers and the necklace, warmed from her skin, slipped lower like a caress. The man caught it before it was lost inside her dress. He tucked it inside his pocket with his other treasures. Even though he now had his prize, he didn't immediately step away.

"That was not so bad, now, was it?" he whispered. His grin

was back. And she realized he didn't scare her. Perhaps he hadn't even scared her when all this had first happened. Was her intuition messing with her or was it steering her in the right direction? She wished she knew.

A dark impulse cascaded through her, and she stepped forward, closing the scant distance between them. He watched her but didn't move to grab her closer nor to evade her.

"You are a bewitching woman," he muttered, seemingly to himself. "Easily the most unusual woman I have met."

"You have no idea." She grinned up at him. The tiny bit of light from the lantern caught on the snowflakes and made them sparkle and dance around them like bubbles in champagne. Her grandmother would have proclaimed it a sign of true Christmas magic. And, for a moment, she wanted to believe in it—that just like time travel was apparently a thing, maybe the magic of Christmas could be real too.

Giddiness erupted through her. Was she really going to do this? Yes. Yes, she was.

Then she did exactly what she'd been tempted to do a few minutes earlier. She rose up and pressed her lips to his. The air between them zinged with energy. His arms closed around her, and it was everything she could have imagined and more. So much more. The world around them seemed to fall away as their mouths and tongues danced together.

She'd never in her life been kissed like this. Was it the hint of danger making it so mesmerizing? Or was it something else?

And then it was over.

The highwayman panted lightly as he gazed down at her. She had done that to him, made him breathless. It felt like a victory.

"You, my lady, are dangerous." He lifted her hand to his

and kissed her wrist. "Take care. You know not who you tempt."

He stepped away from her just as a noise behind her made her spin around. Another man stepped out of the carriage. What the—? He'd been in there with Alice. She scowled at the man and clenched her hands into fists.

"Did you hurt her?" she demanded.

The new man looked startled. "Never."

Even in that one word, she caught the difference in his accent. This man was Scottish. Well, that was something identifiable, not that she planned to report the robbery, even if that was what any normal person would do.

"I'm fine, Cassy," Alice called out from inside the carriage. "Please, come back inside. I'm freezing."

The two men dipped their heads at Cassy, then mounted their horses. A third man emerged on horseback from the other side of the carriage.

"Your driver is fine," the third man said as he rode by to catch up with his companions. "And thank you for your generosity." He dipped his head in acknowledgement. "Until next time, ladies."

As the men disappeared into the trees along the dark, snowy road, Cassy jumped into action. She'd forgotten all about the driver. She raced around the carriage and found the man leaning against a large, spoked wheel with his arms bound with rope. It was the limo driver who'd picked her up from her house, although his attire had been similarly changed to match this era.

"Are you okay?" she asked as she picked at the loose knot until it came free. It took longer than it should have because her fingers were numb with cold.

"Yes, yes," he said impatiently.

How could she still be thinking about the highwayman's

kiss, wishing it had been longer, wishing they'd been somewhere private, when this poor man had been bound and threatened at gunpoint?

She'd officially lost her mind. Maybe she needed a sign made up to hang around her neck: Here stands Cassy Tilbury, the most ridiculous person in the world.

CHAPTER 4

Like magic, if love is meant to be,
it will not be ignored.
Grandma Lucy's Rules to Magic and Dating

Nestled against a forested backdrop, the little stone cottage with its thatched roof and overgrown garden had an untamed, whimsical quality to it that remained even in the dead of winter. If this place still existed two hundred some odd years from now, it was undoubtedly a very popular tourist stop. Cassy could easily see people circling it to find just the right place to take their selfies.

At the moment, though, all Cassy wanted to do was get inside and shove her feet close to a roaring fire. Well, maybe that wasn't all she wanted. She also wanted to find out what had happened to Alice. Considering how scared the woman had been when they'd first been stopped on the side of the road, she was remarkably relaxed about the whole thing by the end of it.

The driver carried their trunks inside the little house, then started a fire in the hearth. When he moved to leave with the carriage, Cassy stopped him.

"I'm fine, ma'am," he said. "I have my own place to stay, I promise. I will return to pick you up for the ball."

Who was this guy? Had he really travelled through time with them just to end up as a servant? That sounded like a terrible way to spend the holiday, but there wasn't much for Cassy to do except let the man leave.

Alice was the bigger priority.

Cassy managed to wait until they were settled in the small parlor with a cup of hot tea before she pounced.

"Okay," Cassy said. "Out with it. What happened with that guy in the carriage?"

Alice blinked at her. Her forehead wrinkled as if she didn't understand what Cassy was asking. Right. Like Cassy was going to believe that.

"Hmm? I don't know—"

"Cut the crap, Alice. Who was that guy?" She narrowed her eyes at her companion, whose cheeks were getting redder by the second. "Oh, wow. You know him, don't you?"

Alice squeaked. Actually squeaked.

"I didn't see that coming," Cassy said. "Tell me about him." Did Alice know the other highwayman too? Was there a way for Cassy to see him again?

"I really don't know what you are talking about." Alice sipped daintily at her tea, but her calm façade wasn't fooling Cassy.

"It must be someone you've met before, which means you've crossed paths with him on some of your other travels."

"No comment."

"That's as good as a confirmation, you know."

Alice frowned.

"But you'd said you'd never been in this era before." Cassy rubbed her chin. What did that mean? Was the guy another time traveling witch? Or someone who lived a really long time? What other types of paranormal people were out there in the world? Her grandmother had told her stories, if only she could remember them. "Is he a vampire or something?"

"How did you figure that out?" The tea in Alice's cup sloshed over the side as she dropped it on the side table. The cup clattered against the saucer.

"Vampires are real? Wow. I don't even know why I'm surprised at this point. I'm mean we're hanging out in another century. It's just... yeah. That's something."

"Why don't you know this stuff?" Alice asked. "You're a witch. I tested your magic. And yet you act like a mundane who doesn't know magic exists."

"I have magic?"

Alice snorted. "Like you don't know."

"Actually, I don't," Cassy said quietly. She stared into the flames dancing in the fire. "I was raised by my grandmother, but she died when I was just a kid. She..." Cassy swallowed. "She used to talk about magic, but as I got older, I thought her stories were just fairytales."

"Gina is going to kill me for this. I was so sure..." Alice's words trailed off as she groaned and slumped in her chair.

"Yeah. I guess you shouldn't really drag people through time unless they are in the know about all things supernatural, hey?"

"Something like that," Alice muttered.

"And the guy?"

Alice dropped her head back and stared at the ceiling. "He... I don't even know what to say about him. I've known Duncan since I was eight when I traveled through time for the first time. It was an accident. I had no idea what had happened, but there he was, all scraped knees and ginger hair, ready to protect me and take me home like a stray cat he'd found on the side of the road. I knew in that moment we'd be friends. Of course, that was before he was changed."

"Changed?"

"Into a vampire." Alice rubbed her arms. "I guess I should have known he'd be here. He's always around when I travel some place."

Cassy leaned back in her chair and stared at the fire. "So, you're friends with one of the highwaymen. Interesting."

"He isn't usually a thief. I don't know what he's doing with those men. He is one of the most morally black and white people I know." Alice's cheeks darkened as she defended him. "But, yeah, I guess we're friends." She sighed. "It isn't like we can be anything else. It isn't like we can build a life together. Witches and vampires. Yeah. Our kind don't mix."

"Romeo-and-Juliet kind of don't mix or are there compatibility issues that I don't understand."

"I mean his whole life is in a different time. But then there is my family too. They just wouldn't accept someone like him." Her mouth turned down and tears glistened in her eyes. She blinked them away quickly. "I'm going to turn in for the night."

Family sucked sometimes. As much as Cassy wanted to urge Alice to not let other people dictate her life, she knew it wasn't always that easy.

"Yeah, okay," Cassy said. "You know if you ever want to talk, I'm here for you."

Alice nodded, then left to find her room.

Well, that would suck. Being in love with someone and not knowing how to find a way to be together? It was probably just as well Cassy didn't know how to find the highwayman again. Not that she believed in love at first sight, but her intuition, which she now thought might be her magic speaking, said that by getting to know the highwayman, she'd be risking far more than a few pieces of jewelry.

And she wasn't sure her heart could handle being broken again.

CHAPTER 5

Most Tilbury women like their men like they like their coffee:
strong, magically blessed, and (almost) too hot to handle.
Grandma Lucy's Rules to Magic and Dating

A ball. A real ball.

Cassy's excitement upon seeing the beautifully dressed men and women was almost enough to eclipse her persistent wish to hunt down the highwayman and kiss him again. Her own magically supplied dress, which was a gorgeous deep blue taffeta with intricately embroidered detailing, was equal to any of those parading in front of her. Alice, who was turning out to be Cassy's very own fairy godmother, was doing an excellent job of supplying everything Cassy could want, right down to the new jeweled combs and necklaces, which Cassy had found nestled amongst the clothes in her trunk. She grinned. If the highwayman saw her now, he'd wish he'd searched her trunks.

And there she was, thinking about that man again.

But it didn't matter. By the end of the night, her head

would be so full of elegant dresses and elaborate decorations she wouldn't even remember what his wicked grin looked like.

As soon as she stepped into the ballroom, Cassy gasped at how enchanting it all was. Boughs of greenery were hung along the walls. Candles flickered from every corner. And the musicians at the far end of the hall were playing a lively song that had dancers reeling over the open area in the middle of the room.

"Wow."

"Isn't it wonderful?" Alice looped her arm through Cassy's. "Lady Rowley still follows many of the older Georgian traditions, but her grandchildren insist on livening things up with some more modern touches too. It's a marvelous mix."

"More modern touches?"

Alice leaned in. "I shouldn't be surprised if we hear a waltz tonight. It's still considered quite scandalous at Almack's and such."

"How do you remember all of these things? You said you'd never been in this time before."

Alice shrugged. "It's part of my magic. I don't usually remember the details when I return to my primary timeline, but I know enough when I travel that I can sidestep most problems."

"Not that I'm planning to mingle much, but do we need introductions?" Wasn't that a thing in all those historical novels? If they did, that would be a problem, since she didn't know anyone but Alice.

"Not at a private event like this. Everyone is considered introduced already." Alice squeezed Cassy's arm. "Oh, look. They've hung kissing balls."

Uh, kissing balls? "Like mistletoe?"

"Exactly like that."

And yep, there she was thinking about the highwayman

and that kiss again. Cassy eyed the globe-shaped bunches of greenery hanging from the ceiling. With holly, ivy, mistletoe and bits of pine trees all put together in a big ball, it was far more elaborate than the sprig of mistletoe hung up by a ribbon that her grandmother used to use.

"That's, uh, nice." She couldn't even glance at them without butterflies dive-bombing through her stomach. She forced herself to look away. It would probably be safer if she didn't go anywhere near the kissing balls. "So, now what happens?"

"We should mingle."

Cassy nodded. Okay. She could do that. Nothing that happened here would follow her back home, just like a weekend in Vegas. It could be fun to pretend to be the wicked widow.

"Remember what we talked about this afternoon," Alice whispered. "Since you're pretending to be a widow from New York, you'll have more flexibility in how you behave, but it might be best to keep conversations to neutral topics to start. What did Elizabeth say in *Pride and Prejudice*? Talk about the dance, the size of the room, or the number of couples."

Cassy laughed.

Curious gazes were following them now. Mostly men. Mostly looking at Cassy and her fashionably low-cut dress rather than Alice in her much more conservative gown, which befitted her role as a spinster. It was strange to be the object of curiosity. Through most of her everyday life, she just blended in. People were too busy on their cell phones or avoiding making eye contact to really pay much attention to the people around them.

Within minutes, a few men approached them. Within half an hour, people seemed to know their names and the lies they'd shared about their lives. Within an hour, Cassy had turned down more offers to dance than she'd ever received in her life. It wasn't that she didn't want to dance, but she didn't know the steps. She appeased her disappointment with tapping her foot, where no one could see it under her gown.

The only things to draw more gossip than their arrival at the ball were tales of highwaymen. It seemed nearly everyone had either been held up or knew of someone who had. The men were disgusted by the situation, complaining about the mob who'd attacked them at gunpoint. Hordes of thieves set upon their carriage in the dead of night, didn't you know? And the women fluttered their fans and looked ready to faint. Smelling salts were passed around like cocaine in an eighty's movie about drug cartels. But under the fluttering and the sniffing, Cassy recognized the excitement and the barely concealed thrill of having been exposed to the highwaymen. Something dark twisted through her at the thought of *her* highwayman luring other women into the shadows and kissing them too.

"Excuse me for a minute," Alice whispered to Cassy.

"Is something the matter?" Was Alice thinking the same thing about Duncan?

"I'm fine." Alice shook her head, but the flush in her cheeks betrayed her lie. Cassy frowned, but it wasn't like she could block the other woman from leaving.

As soon as Alice stepped away, an unfamiliar sense of vulnerability settled over Cassy. Alice was her tether in this place. Cassy didn't know how to survive here without the other woman. She could only pray Alice returned quickly. Luckily, no one was hanging about her at the moment. Maybe she could just find her way to where the wallflowers were clustered and hide away until Alice returned. There were always wallflowers, right? At least there were in every historical romance novel she'd ever read.

Cassy scanned the room. A tall man with dark red hair, wide shoulders, and very pale skin was stalking through the crowd on the other side of the room. His eyes never left Alice as she made her way to one of the doors. That had to be Duncan. Wow. Cassy could definitely see the appeal.

Did that mean her highwayman was here too?

Cassy's heart quickened at the idea.

A man with brown hair and a roguish glint in his dark eyes stepped close, obstructing her view. Startled by his nearness, she took a step back. There was something familiar about him, which was crazy talk because she certainly had never met anyone here before.

Oh, wait.

Her gaze darted over the man's neatly aligned teeth, his smooth cheeks and his perfectly shaped chin.

Then the man smiled, and her heart tripped over itself, because standing in front of her was none other than her highwayman. And he looked good... much, much too good for a guy who robbed people under the cloak of darkness. His mouth quirked in that telltale smirk of his and she knew he knew she knew. Her mouth went dry. What would he do to her?

"Mrs. Tilbury, we meet again."

"I see my reputation precedes me," she managed to say, sounding entirely too breathless. It wasn't surprising that he had heard her name. It seemed everyone here had at this point in the evening. "And now I fear you have me at a disadvantage"

"May I have this dance?" He extended his hand to her, in a move reminiscent of the night they'd met. His grin widened. He knew exactly what he was doing.

She'd turned down dance offers all night, so she knew she should say no to him too—propriety demanded it, right?—but the idea of being close to this man was too much temptation. She *had* to say yes. But how would she survive the dance itself? She didn't know how to dance a quadrille or a reel or a cotillion. Worse, she didn't even know what those songs sounded like.

"I, umm... It has been some time since I danced," she stammered. "I'm sure I've forgotten the steps."

"I believe this one will be easy enough. All you have to do is follow my lead. I promise I will not steer you wrong."

And that's when she heard the familiar strains of a waltz starting up. Around her, the ladies tittered. Hadn't Alice said there was nothing quite as scandalous as a waltz? But at least she knew the steps to this one. It was one of the dances everyone learned in school and then refreshed before their weddings. Even if the steps had changed a bit over the years, it was at least a familiar beat.

"It is a private ball, Mrs. Tilbury. It is not like we are dancing at Almack's. The rules are a little more relaxed here." He leaned closer. Mischief danced in his dark eyes. Under the candlelight she could see they were a rich brown color. "Please, do not disappoint me now. Do you know what I had to promise to both the host and the orchestra to make this happen?"

"Your promises are not my concern, Mr....?" But even as she rebuked his attempt to goad her into dancing, she let herself be led onto the dance floor.

"Mr. Graham Everton." He dipped his head. "It is a pleasure to make your acquaintance."

He pulled her into his arms, and it was like the last twenty-four hours evaporated and she was standing in his arms at the side of the snowy road, kissing him again. His right hand, concealed in a pristine white glove tonight, rested lightly at her waist, while his other wrapped loosely around her own. Despite the distance between their bodies, it felt very much like an intimate embrace.

They circled the room as he expertly guided her through the surprisingly large number of dancers. If her fingers tightened on his muscular shoulder, just to feel the way his body moved beneath her hand... well, who would know?

"I wondered if I would see you tonight," he murmured.

"I wondered the same thing." She didn't bother trying to lie. Besides, in a few days, she wouldn't be here any longer. She didn't have time to play at being coy. "Are you worried that I know who you are?"

One of his eyebrows rose. "And what do you know, Mrs. Tilbury?"

"Do you kiss all of the women you hold up at gunpoint?" She flushed. That was the last thing she should have said, but somehow the question just leapt from her mouth.

He leaned his head in, so it was close to her ear. So much like he'd done on the night he'd stopped their carriage. His warm breath fanned over her exposed neck in a teasing caress. "I believe, Mrs. Tilbury, that it was you who kissed me."

Cassy had nothing to say to that, but her cheeks heated. She wasn't a virginal young debutante from this era, though. Why was she blushing at the thought of a kiss when she could easily imagine doing so much more with him? As a self-proclaimed widow, she wasn't expected to be too prim and proper, was she? Hmm... How *did* people set up assignations?

"How does no one recognize you?" His disguise was only a short step up from Clark Kent's glasses.

His shoulder rolled in a little shrug. "People see what they wish to see. They would never imagine one of their peers would do such a thing, so they see things as they are not."

That was probably true.

"Does it worry you?" He eyed her carefully as he waited for her answer.

"Not as much as it probably should." She bit her bottom lip at her admission. His gaze caught on her mouth and his breath seemed to hitch.

"You look flushed, my dear," he whispered. His voice sounded rougher and deeper than it had a moment earlier. "Do you need to step away from the crowd for a moment?"

Her gaze locked with his and she nodded. "Yes. I think I do."

CHAPTER 6

Books are a form of magic,
so libraries are places of joy.
Grandma Lucy's Rules to Magic and Dating

With a devilish grin, he immediately guided them to the edge of the dance floor. They had just stepped into the group of people mingling along the perimeter of the room when the orchestra finished the final refrains of the waltz. No one seemed to notice as they wove their way to one of the room's doorways.

Cassy barely spared Alice a thought as they slipped into the dimly lit hallway, but if Alice could sneak away, so could Cassy.

Mr. Everton, or rather Graham, because she couldn't keep thinking of the man so formally after the kiss they'd shared, slipped his hand in hers as he led Cassy down the hallway. He seemed to know exactly where to go. Considering how many people were in attendance, Cassy was surprised they didn't come across anyone else on their trek through the house. Their route twisted and turned and went up a couple of steps and twisted again. She'd never been in such a large house before.

"How do you know where to go?"

Graham didn't answer. Instead, he finally stopped in front of a door and ushered her inside. The room was a breathtaking realization of every bibliophile's dream: wall to wall bookshelves overladen with leather bound tomes, a long settee finished with a rich golden fabric, and a heavy ornate desk and chair off to one side of the room. Absolutely stunning. Any minute now she could break into song and swing from the library ladder like Belle in *Beauty and the Beast*.

The door clicked shut behind her, followed by the scrape of a key in a lock. She spun around to face Graham. He was even more impressive than the library, and that was saying something.

"You never answered my question," she said. "Is this your home?"

Graham choked out a laugh and ducked his chin. "In my dreams. No, sadly, I am only the son of a bankrupt baron."

"Fair enough. Someone with this much wealth should have no need to steal from women."

His ever-present grin faltered. "I wish I could say it was all for a lark, but..." He shrugged. "Alas, we each have burdens we must carry."

"Why did you bring me here?"

"Why did you come with me?"

She turned away from him and walked to the nearest bookshelf. The gilt lettering glinted under the glow of the candles on the desk. "Did you come here earlier and set out the candles? Maybe even unlock the door?"

"Would you punish me for being hopeful?"

"You could have any woman in that ballroom tonight,

particularly if they knew of your clandestine nightly activities. Why me?"

"I could say the same about you. I saw the way men were looking at you." His footsteps were muffled against the thick Persian rug as he closed the distance between them. Then he moved even closer, until she could feel his front against her back. Solid. Warm. His hands rested lightly on her hips. She should feel trapped. Instead, she felt deliciously tempted to lean back and encourage him to do more. His lips grazed the side of her neck. "Do you wish for me to shower you with compliments? Talk about the exquisite beauty of your complexion or the luster of your hair? Perhaps mention how the color of your eyes reminds me of the sky on a winter's morning?"

She shivered and gave into the urge to tilt her head, giving him more access to her neck. "Those all sound very practiced and bland."

He huffed out a soft laugh. "And yet, they are all true. But the real reason is I could not stop thinking about you. Your demands for promises of safety intrigued me. Your fearlessness when stepping outside of that carriage entranced me. And your kiss... Your kiss has haunted me. I am sure I have thought of nothing else since."

"Our kiss haunted me too," she whispered.

He turned her gently in his arms until they were facing one another again. "What is your given name?"

"Cassy. Short for Cassandra."

"My friends call me Gray."

"Are we friends?"

"I hope we will be so much more," he whispered. "May I kiss you, Cassy?"

Cassy laughed. "I am sorry I didn't think to ask your permission the last time we met."

His gaze dipped to her lips, and she wanted nothing more than to feel his mouth against hers again.

"Yes, Gray," she whispered. "I would like you to kiss me."

The kiss started soft and sweet. A brush of lips. A whisper of breath shared between them. A tightening of his fingers on her hips. Her hands slid up his body until she could wrap her arms around his neck to pull him closer. His warmth enveloped her. The woodsy scent of him teased her senses. He tasted of the punch that had been served at the ball and she wanted to kiss him until all that was gone and all that remained were whatever decadent flavors were uniquely his alone. As their kiss deepened, they pressed together more tightly. Her chest to his. His hips to hers. His hands moved up and down her back in long sensuous strokes as she arched against him. They were fully clothed, but the way her body flared to life was anything but innocent.

The grandfather clock in the corner of the room ticked away the minutes as they lost themselves in one another. Between those sweet kisses, they talked—about everything really. Although there were things about her life that wouldn't make sense to him, there were a lot of things they could discuss: a love of reading, an appreciation for the outdoors, a dream of connecting with another person...

When the clock chimed the hour, the clang startled Cassy, and the kisses and the conversation ended. Gray lifted his hand to her throat and caressed her racing pulse with one of his gloved fingers. Could he feel the rush of her blood through the fabric? She thought about making a joke about him reaching for her jewels again, but it didn't feel right, seeming crass somehow.

"If we do not leave now, we will miss the dinner."

Cassy didn't care about dinner, but maybe Gray did. This was his life. His real one. She couldn't harm his standing in this world. Although she thought men likely enjoyed more liberties than women in this era, there were still probably complex social mores to follow. She would be gone in a few days, but he had to stay here.

And didn't that just feel like a punch to the gut?

Even her intuition, or magic as she was slowly starting to think of it, bucked at the idea of leaving this man behind. But what could she do? She was merely a visitor. And it wasn't like love at first sight existed. That was something that only existed in fairytales.

A bit like magic and vampires and witches were fairytales too?

Except Gray wasn't in love with her. And she couldn't figure out what she felt about him. Given everything, this couldn't be anything more than just a little interlude in their lives.

"Yes." She cleared her throat. "We should return to the ball."

CHAPTER 7

Always look for the man who protects those around him.
He is the one who will be worthy of you.
Grandma Lucy's Rules to Magic and Dating

The orchestra had stopped playing music by the time they returned to the ballroom and people were arranging themselves to make the procession into the dinner. Gray stood close to her but hadn't held her hand since they had left the library. She missed the heat and connection. She also missed the feel of his lips moving against hers, but that wasn't going to happen again anytime soon either.

He winked at her, like he knew what she was thinking.

A man who looked a lot like Gray came rushing up to them. A brother maybe?

"Where were you?" The man's eyes darted over Cassy, widening slightly as if he knew who she was.

"Why?" Gray frowned at the new arrival.

"Our father." His whispered voice broke and his face paled. "He is insisting on an announcement and demanded that I find you. I..." His words trailed off.

Gray nodded sharply and his mouth flattened into a grim line, as if he knew exactly what his brother was trying to say and didn't like it one bit. "That is not going to happen."

"Lottie is distraught, but I don't know how to help her. Or you," the man said furtively. He glanced at Cassy, like he wasn't sure he wanted all this aired in front of her, but the situation was too dire to do anything else.

Gray gripped his brother's shoulder tightly. His jaw was set, and his nostrils flared. Whatever was going on wasn't good. Had someone discovered their late-night activities? Because Cassy suspected this man had to be the third rider who'd accosted them on the road.

Then Gray narrowed his eyes at something over Cassy's shoulder. She glanced in that direction and saw Alice standing in the doorway. She looked completely adrift in a sea of strangers. Her eyes were red and swollen, like she'd been crying.

Cassy pushed her way toward Alice, who seemed relieved to see her approach. Although she looked less impressed when Gray followed her. She dragged Alice into a quiet corner of the hallway where they were partially shielded by a large potted plant.

"Please, go," she said to Gray. "Your brother needs you."

He shook his head and didn't leave. Gray scanned their surroundings, like he was assessing the area for threats. She found the whole thing oddly touching.

"What happened?" she asked Alice. "Are you hurt?"

"I have to leave," Alice sputtered. "I just can't... I can't stay here."

"Of course," Cassy said. She shot an apologetic look at Gray, hoping he understood. "Let's collect our cloaks and we'll ditch this joint."

"I will arrange for your carriage to be brought around," Gray said, then his gaze drifted upward.

Cassy looked up too. Her breath caught when she saw they were standing under one of those kissing balls. What in the world was it doing out here? Then Gray was stepping closer. He paused for a moment as their gazes caught. Her heart raced at the hope and longing she saw reflected in his eyes. In that moment, all the candlelight seemed to catch on every bit of jeweled or gilt surface in the room and the air around them sparkled. It could have been magic. Maybe it was. When their mouths met, it was a mere brush of lips but in that moment, it felt like the world filled with joy and wonder.

Could a kiss be deemed a Christmas miracle? Because something seemed to shift inside her and suddenly the world seemed beautiful and pure and perfect.

And then he was gone, stepping away from her. He spun on his heel and disappeared into the crowd.

In less than half an hour, Cassy and Alice were bundled into the carriage and being jostled down the road to the cottage. Gray had been exceedingly proper through the whole ordeal, while Cassy wished she could press her lips to his one last time in farewell. But that would have probably been too much for this crowd, even if she was playing a potentially wicked widow.

As soon as the manor house slipped out of sight, Cassy crossed the carriage and sat beside Alice. She wrapped her arms around the other woman.

"What happened, Alice? Please let me help."

Alice's only response was to sob into Cassy's shoulder.

By the time they arrived at the cottage, Cassy still didn't know what had occurred to upset Alice, but it didn't take a genius to figure out a certain redheaded vampire was likely to blame. And here she was without any wooden stakes.

Alice still refused to talk even after she was settled in front of a crackling fire and with a fresh cup of tea poured for her.

"I am here if you want to talk," Cassy offered.

Alice merely nodded and twisted a square bit of fabric around her fingers. She swallowed loudly. "I... I need to leave. I am so sorry."

"I understand. I can have everything packed and ready to go in a flash."

Alice's face contorted in horror. "No. You must stay. It is your holiday."

"I can't stay without you."

"Of course, you can. Everything is arranged. You don't need to worry about anything. Food, clothing, money. It's all taken care of. Take a walk in the village. Go skating. There is so much to do."

"Alice, I don't think—"

"You can't leave without saying goodbye to Mr. Everton."

"Gray doesn't matter. I will never see him again anyway." Cassy rubbed absently at her chest, which grew pained at the idea of leaving him.

"I was never really supposed to be here," Alice whispered. "I just sort of crashed your holiday. Please, don't make this worse for me. I already feel guilty enough."

Cassy leaned back in her chair and studied the dancing flames. What would she do if she stayed? She was unlikely to cross paths with Gray again, but she wasn't ready to return to her dreary life and her too quiet house again so soon either.

"Here, take this," Alice said as she extended her hand. On her palm lay a shiny gold ring. Cassy picked it up. Nothing about it was particularly remarkable. "You don't need me to see you safely back home. At the end of your holiday, you will simply be returned there. No fuss. No glitter." She gestured to the ring. "But if you decide you want to return sooner than that, all you have to do is wish on that ring."

"Like Dorothy's red shoes? Click my heels together three times and wish for home?"

"Yes, I suppose. I've never actually seen that movie, but it sounds about right. Just make sure you're touching the ring when you make the wish."

"What about the limo guy?"

"Jim? Oh, he's already moved on. You won't see him again."

"Oh. I didn't realize that." Cassy fidgeted with the ring. "Are you sure you don't want to talk about this? Maybe try to find Duncan and work out whatever's happened?"

Alice pursed her lips and crossed her arms. Now that her tears had stopped, she seemed to be settling into anger. "I don't think that's possible."

Cassy rolled the ring back and forth with her fingers. With a get out of jail card like this, the idea of staying seemed too good to give up. She felt bad for Alice, but she was warming up to the idea of staying here on her own.

"Are you sure I can stay here alone?"

"Of course." Alice waved her hand through the air, dismissing Cassy's worries. "It'll make me happy to know you are still here enjoying your time away."

As if accepting her own words as permission to leave, Alice rushed to her room and threw her belongings into her trunk.

"You can always come back," Cassy said after she gave Alice a hug. "You might change your mind, and that would be okay."

Alice tightened her arms around Cassy. "Thank you,

Cassy. I've enjoyed meeting you and helping you with your holiday. Please don't let this impact how you feel about Gina's Time Travel Agency."

"When I get back, we should meet for coffee. I have a lot of questions." Alice tensed in her arms. "I won't ask about what happened tonight," Cassy rushed to say. "Not if you don't bring it up first. But the magic stuff? I would like to know more about that too."

"Good-bye, Cassy." Alice nodded and pulled out of the hug. She wiped her reddened nose on the balled-up bit of fabric she was still clutching, and then Alice and her trunk disappeared from the room.

CHAPTER 8

Never turn away a gift you want.
Grandma Lucy's Rules to Magic and Dating

The next morning, Cassy lingered in bed under a layer of warm blankets. The air was so chilled in the room she could see her breath. The fire in the grate had died out long ago. The house was completely silent.

How strange not to hear a furnace kick in, the hum of the refrigerator, or the fan in her laptop. There wasn't even the sound of distant car engines or planes flying overhead.

In the summer, the air was probably filled with the sounds of birds and bugs, but on a cold winter's morning, it was eerily quiet. Wasn't there a room somewhere that was so devoid of sound it drove people crazy? Cassy had a better appreciation for how that could happen now.

Maybe it would help to start a fire. At least there would be noise and, equally important, heat.

She pulled the blanket around her body and found her way to the parlor. It was a good thing the place didn't come with any servants. They would likely be horrified to see her traipsing around the place in her bedclothes.

Alice had taught her how to start the fire, and Cassy was absurdly happy she was able to get it going so quickly. Then she made her way to the little kitchen and pulled out a loaf of bread and a chunk of cheese. Not a fancy breakfast, but it would do. After pulling a chair closer to the fire, Cassy settled in to enjoy her food and make a plan.

Seeing Alice's tears had been sobering. Whatever fledgling hopes and dreams she'd started to entertain about a certain highwayman would only lead to heartache if they grew any stronger. She really needed to try to save herself from that.

If it wasn't too late already.

She had wonderful memories of Gray. That had to be enough. Today she would do something else. She rubbed at the persistent ache in her chest and hoped it wouldn't take too long to fade away.

Maybe she'd go to town and see how the average person lived. It was as good a plan as anything else. All she needed to do was follow the lane until she crested the hill and she'd find the town. At least that was what Alice had said the first day they'd arrived. She could figure this out. No problem. Maybe she'd find a bookshop. Whiling away the rest of her vacation days with a good story didn't sound too bad.

Getting dressed and presentable was more of an ordeal on her own, but she managed. She was lucky Alice had stayed as long as she had. Cassy would have been completely befuddled if she'd just been dropped here without any help right from the start. She would never have known what to put on first. It made no sense to her that stays went over a chemise but under a petticoat. Was it a laundry issue? Probably. And really, why did she need stays anyway? Wasn't the joy of empire waistlines that dresses weren't cinched in tight?

But whatever. She did it. And she'd even managed to get her hair under control without her usual products and tools. Not too shabby if she did say so herself.

She was just stepping out of the cottage when the sound of footsteps echoed down the snow-covered lane. Since the lane ended at the cottage, she suspected this visitor was meant for her or Alice. Hopefully it wasn't Duncan. She swallowed and eyed the approaching figure more closely. His hair didn't look red from here, although there wasn't much of it visible under his black top hat. The last thing she wanted to do was face down an angry or upset vampire. But vampires couldn't walk around in sunlight, right? Or was that just a myth? When she got back home, she was going to find out about these things.

The ring Alice had given her was an unfamiliar weight on her index finger, but she rubbed her thumb over it, just to make sure it was still there if she needed to make a quick getaway.

The approaching man wasn't Duncan though. It was Gray. From the new batch of butterflies flitting about her stomach to the zip of electricity zinging along her skin, it was like her whole body was rejoicing at the mere sight of him.

"Good morning, Mrs. Tilbury," he said with a grin when he stepped through the arched gateway into the cottage's dormant and leaf-bare garden.

"Mr. Everton, I wasn't expecting you this morning." She matched his formality as she inclined her head. Although she hadn't heard any noises or seen any movement in the area around the cottage, she supposed it was possible someone might be close enough to hear what they were saying.

"Are you and your companion well after last night?"

"Yes. Thank you." She was touched he would come all this way to check on them, although it wasn't as if he could just send a text. There weren't a lot of other options. Some part of her knew she should send him on his way. It would be the proper thing to do. But she wasn't a woman from this era, so what would it matter if she broke the rules? "Would you like to come inside?"

As soon as they stepped inside, and Gray saw that the parlor was empty, he took her hands in his.

"Are you well?" He spoke quietly. "I was worried at how the evening ended. It was not as I had hoped."

"I am well enough. Alice, though..." Cassy sighed. If Gray was friends with Duncan, did that mean he knew about vampires, witches, and magic? That seemed like a complicated conversation, and she didn't know much herself if he had questions, so she decided to keep her explanation simple. "She packed her bags and left last night."

"She left?" He looked around the room again, as if he didn't believe her. "You are alone here?"

"I have the means to return home without her," Cassy said carefully.

"But you are alone?" His gaze collided with hers.

She nodded.

He groaned in response. "How am I supposed to court you properly when every time I see you, I face temptation after temptation?"

"Court me?"

He huffed out a breath, sounding annoyed. "You see? I cannot even think straight. I came this morning to look in on you and Miss Henry, but I also wanted to ask if you would be amenable to courting. I mean would you allow me to court you?" He laughed and his cheeks darkened. "I cannot even get my words out properly when you look at me like that."

"You don't know me."

He squeezed her hands. "If you had asked me just a few days ago if I would want to court someone, I would have scoffed at the very idea of it. I cannot explain what has changed, except it has. *Everything* has changed. I know this is fast. We have probably shared more kisses than conversation, which I never would have imagined either. You know nothing of me, and I know nothing of you, but I cannot imagine my life with anyone but you. It is as if everything has come into focus, and I see what my life should be. And my life is supposed to include you. I am sure of it."

Cassy's intuition blossomed inside her at his words, telling her that he was right. That they were right for one another. But how could they be? She was leaving in a few days, to return to a place he could never even visit. It was an impossible situation.

"I don't know what to say."

"I should not have said all of that. I know it is too much. But I cannot seem to help myself when I am with you."

"We need to talk."

His face contorted. "Please do not say no. Not yet. Let me show you that I am a good man. Let me explain why I..." He cleared his throat. "Why I..."

"Why you are a highwayman?"

"Yes." He grimaced at the title.

"I am guessing it has to do with your father forcing you and your brother into something."

He lifted his eyebrows in surprise.

"Come, sit. I'll make tea for us. I think we have much to discuss." She shouldn't be doing this. She should have just rejected his proposal to court her, pushed him out the door and been done with it. But she couldn't. She just couldn't.

CHAPTER 9

Magic is magic. Love is love. And sometimes when people
come together it is both magic and love
Grandma Lucy's Rules to Magic and Dating

By the time they were settled on the settee with tea
poured into dainty cups, Cassy's nerves were a wreck.
Gray, on the other hand, looked determined and in control.
She envied him that. His confidence was one of the most
attractive things about him. Well, his smoking hot body and
his ridiculously wicked grin didn't hurt either.

"Although my brother and I have been trying to keep this
information a secret, I expect it will be common knowledge
soon enough."

"Then don't tell me." She put her hand on his forearm.
They'd both removed their gloves and outerwear when she'd
set about making the tea. Suddenly, selfishly, she wished she
could hold his hand and feel the warmth of his fingers tangled
with hers, but that would be a step too far down the scale from
proper lady to brazen hussy, wouldn't it? Or did it really

matter since she was alone with him already? And then there were those kisses they'd shared that suggested she'd already wrecked any chances of being considered proper. But bright morning sunlight seemed to demand more propriety than moonlight.

"I need to tell you because it is the reason for everything else." He inhaled deeply. "I already told you my father has the title of baron, but a title with barely two shillings to rub together is almost useless. My father was the youngest son, and our branch of the family was never meant to have the title. My ambitions, until five years ago, were focused on becoming a professor at Oxford, with the hope that one day I might be elected Vice-Chancellor. I am much more comfortable amid books—" his face contorted in a look of sadness, "—but fate and a series of dreadful accidents have given the barony to my father anyway, and following his death, the title will pass to me. To say our lives have changed completely would be an understatement. He was never trained for the position and has mismanaged everything. Whatever resources that remained after a series of poor investments, he has gambled away."

Cassy opened her mouth to say something, but he shook his head to stop her.

"Please. Let me say all of this. If I stop, I don't know if I'll be able to continue." Gray rubbed his forehead. "I say that a title is *almost* useless because to some people it still has value. People with titles seem to think they are better than everyone else, although I have seen nothing to prove that. It is merely an accident of birth, much like the color of your eyes or who your siblings are." He exhaled slowly and studied his hands, which were clasped in front of him now. "I have only one brother, my twin. You met him last night. We always joke that our birth order was mixed up when we were born. Reg would like nothing more than to be the next baron, while I have come to see it as nothing but an unwanted chore."

Gray was destined to be a baron. Wow. She hadn't seen that coming. Dread swirled through Cassy's stomach and enveloped her, but she waited quietly as he collected his thoughts. She wanted to ask him to stop again, to not tell her anything more, but she couldn't. Even if she was beginning to suspect she wouldn't like what he was going to say.

"My father has decided to sell me and the title to a wealthy industrialist, Mr. Lennox. The businessman has agreed to pay my father's debts if I marry his daughter, and she becomes a titled lady."

She gasped. Gray was engaged to be married? Cassy's chest tightened. "So, you steal to try to pay what he owes."

It was easier to talk about his highwayman gig than his upcoming nuptials. The very idea of Gray marrying someone else made her nauseated.

"Arranged marriages are not unusual in our social circle. Under other circumstances, I may have even agreed to it if it weren't for my brother. And now that I've met you, the idea is even more preposterous." Gray studied Cassy's face, as if trying to gauge how she was responding to what he was saying. "Let me take a step back. Reg is very clever with finances. My father says his activities are unsuitable for a gentleman and has done much to undermine my brother's work. Before the title came to my father, however, Reg had systematically increased our family's meagre wealth, mostly through importing goods. It was through these endeavors that he met Mr. Lennox and began to court his daughter, Charlotte. Everything was going well. I'd never seen my brother so happy." He paused for a moment. "Most of his ventures have been successful, but his last one... the ship was lost."

Cassy's chest tightened.

"You can probably guess the outcome." Gray expelled a shaky breath. "Mr. Lennox didn't accumulate his wealth by being kind or forgiving. The loss of my brother's investment, combined with my father's streak of bad luck at the gaming hells, showed the man how vulnerable we were, and he seized the opportunity to buy a title for his family."

"So now Charlotte is to be... your wife?" She choked out the words.

She hated the idea of anyone having to marry under those circumstances. She knew firsthand how soul crushing it was to be in a loveless marriage, even if hers hadn't started out that way. But she particularly hated to imagine Gray bound to a woman he didn't love. Or any woman that wasn't her, really.

Gray grimaced. "Not if I can help it."

"If he is your twin, could you switch places?" Wasn't that the story line of a bunch of movies and dozens of books?

He shook his head. "You saw him with me last night. Our features are too different for anyone to mistake us for one another."

"Right," Cassy said. "I guess I did know that."

"And therein lies the problem. There is no easy solution." Gray's hands tightened into fists. "I will not marry the woman my brother loves, but I cannot see the woman disgraced either. Although I was able to stop their plans last night, I would not be surprised to find our fathers plotting together and making an announcement without my approval, just to force me to do as they demand. The whole situation is untenable."

Cassy's heart ached, physically ached, like someone had shoved their hand right into her chest and squeezed it.

"Reg became the highwayman on his own, desperate to improve our family's situation, to control something in his life, and to save Lottie from her father's machinations. When I discovered what he was doing, I insisted on helping. The trinkets we steal have made very little impact on our father's debt, but still we try. I keep thinking that if Mr. Lennox did not have that leverage..." Gray's shoulders slumped. "I know Father's gambling is only part of the problem, but it is a significant part. Our situation has improved some since Duncan joined us, but it is still not enough. Every time we pay one of my father's debts, he gambles even more. It is a sickness in him that will destroy us all."

"A bit like whack-a-mole," Cassy muttered aloud.

Gray frowned. "I do not understand. Why would you hit a mole?"

"Never mind." Cassy shook her head. "It was a game I played once. But it sounds like..." She scrambled to think of an analogy he would understand. "Like the monster in Greek mythology, the hydra."

"Cutting off one head to find two more in its place." Gray nodded grimly. "Yes. Very much like that."

"I don't know that I can help much, but you can have any and all jewels in my possession," Cassy said, praying they wouldn't disappear like Cinderella's carriage as soon as she was sent back to the twenty-first century.

"I have not made much of a case for why you should accept my courtship, have I? An impoverished heir who robs people under cover of darkness to escape being bound to a woman he could never love."

Cassy took his hand in hers. "That isn't why I can't accept your proposal."

The pained look on his face almost made her take the words back.

"It isn't because of your father or your brother or how quickly this has all happened," she rushed to say. "And it is not about your... your possible fiancée. It is just that my life, it isn't what you imagine it to be. I can't stay here. I'll be leaving in a few days. I have no choice in the matter."

"I have not asked to court you because of your wealth. Please do not believe that is the case."

She was hardly wealthy, but then again, the gowns and the jewels and even the carriage she'd been given upon arriving here would suggest otherwise. She could see how anyone would come to that conclusion. "Phew, I'm glad that isn't why you're here, because honestly I don't have any money either." Especially not in this era. Everything she had had been given to her by Alice's magic. And although she lived comfortably in her regular life, she was not wealthy by any definition.

Gray snorted then, a strange sort of sound that by the surprised look on his face he didn't make very often. A strangled laugh erupted from him. It pulled a choked and reluctant laugh from her too. And then they were both cackling, all the worry and stress exploding from them in raucous laughter. It was probably better to do that than curl up and sob.

When their laughter eased, Cassy wiped tears from her eyes and then the seriousness of their conversation draped over them again.

"I am sorry," Cassy said. "I wish I could—"

"I understand." Gray waved off her apology. "Truly I do. I just wish things could be different. For all of us."

And it could be, couldn't it? If Cassy could convince Alice to transport Gray to the future... Except Alice wasn't here, and Cassy had no way of getting in touch with her. The ring on her finger could potentially help, but what if it didn't? What if it was programmed just for Cassy?

Of course, Gray would also have to believe it was possible. How could she even explain life in the twenty-first century and make it enticing enough for him to want to leave everything he knew behind? He was to become a baron, for pity's sake. How could she compete with that?

"I cannot marry you," Cassy said finally. "I wish I could. I wish I could fix all of this."

Gray nodded. They shared a pained look for several long moments.

"I will not marry her," Gray said as he stared into her eyes. "I have not promised her anything. There is nothing between us. You believe me, don't you?"

Cassy swallowed as she nodded slightly. She understood what he was saying. He was free. Free to be with her. For the moment at least. "I understand," she whispered.

Her breath caught as Gray leaned forward. Cassy moved to meet him. Their mouths crashed together in a mix of desperation and longing for what could have been.

The memories of the sweet, almost innocent kisses they had shared previously were swept away under a wave of desire, want and need. Gray tore his mouth away from hers and stared into her eyes. The heat of arousal poured through her. Her fingers tingled with the need to touch him, to feel his body moving against hers.

"Please, Gray," she murmured as she pressed closer to him.

"Are you sure, Cassy? I would never ask something like that of you. Your reputation..." He looked around the room, as if expecting a scowling chaperone to pop out from behind a chair. "Already I am putting you at risk."

"Gray," she whispered, and pulled his attention back. She held his gaze for a moment. "I want to be with you, Gray.

Always. But we can't have that, so I will take this moment with you and every other moment from now until I have to leave," she said. If they couldn't have forever, they could at least have this. It would have to be enough.

And then he was picking her up and carrying her through the little cottage to the bedroom she'd claimed on her first night here.

CHAPTER 10

Fate has a way of bringing the right people into your life.
You just need to trust its magic.
Grandma Lucy's Rules to Magic and Dating

The late morning sunlight danced over tiny specks of dust, making them sparkle, and cast the bedroom in a soft, intimate warmth, despite the chill in the air. Not that there was any question of why they were there, but Cassy's heart thumped faster at the sight of the bed, which filled most of the room. Gray's eyes were dark and heated as he lowered her to the soft, smooth linens. He sat on the bed beside her and brushed a few stray strands of hair from where they'd fallen across her face. The faint brush of his fingers over her skin made her crave more.

"You are so beautiful," he murmured.

"So are you." Whatever words she could offer wouldn't be enough. But it wasn't just his looks that drew her to him. He made her wish she had a strong magic of her own so she could steal him away from here and be with him forever.

"Do not worry, love, I do not need your compliments and

your praises," he said, as if reading her thoughts. "And I will not ask again if you are sure this is what you want. I trust you know your own heart like I know mine."

She almost couldn't handle the tender way he gazed at her. They shouldn't exchange words like that. It felt too much like something they couldn't have. Something like love. Wasn't that the first rule of one-night stands? Keep your emotional distance?

Oh, the lies she told herself.

But her heart wouldn't survive any more declarations, so Cassy took control by crawling into Gray's lap. The skirt on her dress bunched up around her hips as she straddled his thick, powerful thighs. His arms immediately came around her to ensure she would not fall. She would seize this moment and savor it. This moment wasn't the time for regrets or anticipation of future heartache. She needed to share joy and happiness. It'd been so long since she'd felt any of that, and Gray had given her that and more. They grinned at one another. It was a grin of promise and excitement and that same growing, um, *affection* she was trying to pretend wasn't there.

"Hello," she said softly.

"Hello," he replied gamely.

Then she reached forward with her surprisingly tremulous hands and began gently untying his cravat. He swallowed hard and his Adam's apple bobbed, as her fingers brushed along his smoothly shaven neck. She couldn't stop. She had to see him. She had to feel his skin beneath her hands and his body against hers. By the time the neck cloth hung open and his collar was loosened, they were both breathing quickly. Seeing him just a little bit undone was enough to make her heart race. She bit her bottom lip as intimacy wove around them like a spell.

If only they could share a thousand more similar moments.

"Your turn," she murmured. The audacious version of herself, the one who had crawled into Gray's lap a few minutes earlier, had apparently scampered off now, leaving Cassy feeling strangely exposed despite her still being fully clothed.

His breath hitched at her words, but his hands slid up her body to comply with her request. His hands didn't tremble as much as hers, but they were still unsteady as he plucked at the short row of buttons on the bodice of her dress. Then he drew the gown over her head and cast it aside. She still wore more than she did during the summer back home, but it didn't feel like it at the moment. Her nerves fluttered in awareness at being both strangely exposed and yet not bare enough, all at the same time. How many more layers to go? Too many. She felt like one of those Christmas presents with seventy-five layers of wrapping paper and tape. Those ones that took an hour and the use of a pair of scissors before you could get to the good stuff.

Gray's palms settled on her hips again instead of moving on to the buttons on her petticoat, as if he was consciously trying to savor this moment by making it last as long as possible. Desire cascaded through her under the heat and weight of his palms. She undulated against him, needing to feel more of his strength and warmth.

"You are more enchanting every time I look upon you," he muttered, seemingly to himself. His fingers tightened on her, as if to assure himself she was really in his arms.

Their mouths collided as they moved toward each other once more. Desire tangled with urgency as the kiss deepened. Any earlier restraint was lost under their growing need for one another. Instead of carefully peeling off layer by layer of clothing, their hands pushed forcefully at garments, their fingers fumbled eagerly at clasps and ties, and their mouths frantically claimed each bit of skin as it was exposed, until their flushed bodies were bare. She wanted to commit every bit of this moment to memory, starting with the way his body felt against hers with nothing between them. Hands stroked unabashedly over skin, reveling in each discovery and shiver of delight. As their explorations quickened and their touches grew bolder, there was a rightness between them, as if some ancient deity had given their blessing to this moment, to the two of them coming together. Cassy had never felt anything like this before. It certainly hadn't been anything like this with her ex. And, instinctively, she knew it'd never be like this with anyone but Gray.

Then she froze.

Reality crashed over her. They didn't have protection. Sure, she'd had her birth control shot, but it wasn't like the condoms she'd packed had arrived in her trunk. And, even if Alice's magic had given her a nineteen-century equivalent, she wasn't sure she would even want to try it.

But, as foolish as it was, especially considering that even in this era sex had its share of diseases, she didn't want to stop. Gray would only be hers for these few days. She wanted him, no matter the risks. Still, she should ask, right?

He was trailing kisses from her ear to her shoulder when she cleared her throat.

"Have you, um...?"

He paused and looked at her.

"Do you have a lover? Or have you, um, been with many people? Intimately?"

"Do not worry. I will please you." He grinned, then leaned forward to resume tasting her skin.

"No. That's, um, not it." She shook her head. He paused

and looked at her again. She swallowed. What could she say that would make sense to him? "My, um, my husband's brother..." Yes, that was it. "When my husband's brother became ill, I overheard his valet talking. He said it was because he'd been with a lover who, um, had some kind of infection. I just..."

Heat burned her cheeks. Could this be any more awkward? This conversation was so much easier in the twenty-first century. Maybe because everyone expected it and could talk about test results before breaking out a pack of condoms.

"Oh, I see," Gray said. Thankfully, he didn't seem put off by her question, though his cheeks darkened as he realized what she was asking. "I had a few—" he cleared his throat, "—trysts when I was younger. But since my father gained his title, my time has been spent trying to fix his various messes. I do not have the inclination or energy for such diversions. I have not taken anyone to my bed for a long time. I do not believe I have any disease that would harm you, or I would not be here with you now. I would never do anything to knowingly hurt you."

"I haven't been with anyone since my husband," Cassy said, feeling she needed to share with him too. She couldn't exactly tell Gray that she'd demanded her doctor test her for everything under the sun after her ex's numerous affairs had come to light, and that everything had come back fine, but she thought it was only fair to reassure him anyway. "And I don't have any concerns either.

"Do you want to continue?"

She nodded. Yes. She wanted that and more.

He smiled and brushed his lips across hers softly as they stretched across the bed, hip to hip and chest to chest. Their legs entwined, their tongues danced together, then they became lost in each other in a rush of heat and caresses and moans. While her hands stroked over the planes of his muscular body and explored each rise and hollow, he caressed each of hers, returning to those places that made her quiver and gasp over and over again.

"Please, Gray, now," she whispered against his kiss.

Her name fell from his lips as they moved against one another. When his body finally joined with hers, such profound happiness stole over her that she laughed with the joy of it. She wanted to live in this moment for the rest of her life.

CHAPTER 11

Magic demands honesty
and so do relationships.
Grandma Lucy's Rules to Magic and Dating

As Cassy snuggled closer to Gray, she wished she never had to leave his arms. The cottage wasn't luxurious, but it was perfect for what they needed. Food supplies were limited to tea, bread, cheese and apples, but they had enough to last for several days, so they wouldn't starve. Yes, she could happily hibernate here, perfectly content and safe, until she had to leave.

The rest of the world could take care of itself.

When they weren't discovering all the wonderful secrets about each other's bodies, they talked. They didn't always understand one another's slang or expressions, but it didn't matter because the sense of rightness between them continued to grow and blossom. She just wished she didn't have to edit out so much of her life, but she didn't know how to explain to a man from this era that she had a job and a house of her own. Or even talk about her previous relationships and how her ex had married again before the ink was even dry on their stupid divorce papers.

Morning faded into afternoon, afternoon coasted into evening, and one day drifted into the next until it was the night before she was scheduled to return. Alice hadn't come back, so any hope of extending her time here was gone.

But she couldn't be sad. Not about meeting Gray. She just wished she had something to give him. The perfect Christmas gift. Something he could remember her by.

Her gaze drifted over to the ring Alice had given her. It lay on the table beside the bed, glinting in the candlelight. Would Gray even believe her if she told him the truth? Or would she just destroy their last hours together?

She had to try. Her intuition—her magic?—demanded it.

Blankets were tucked tightly around them as they simply held one another. Cassy lifted her head from where it rested on Gray's naked shoulder, breaking apart their safe cocoon. She propped herself on her elbow and forced herself to meet his eyes. After so many days exploring one another, his face and body were as familiar to her as her own.

"What is the matter?"

"There is something I need to tell you," she began slowly. "I'm scared of how you'll react."

"You hold my secrets," he said. "I would be honored if you shared yours with me in return."

"This is going to sound crazy, but I need you to trust me."

He narrowed his eyes, as if trying to figure out what kind of secret would warrant such an introduction, before nodding slowly. Then he sat up and leaned against the headboard. "Does this have to do with where you come from? It is not New York, is it?"

"How did you know?"

Gray shrugged. "I have met a few Americans. At first, I

thought you sounded like them, but the more I have heard you talk the more I see the differences. You are unlike anyone I have ever met. Especially since you are a woman."

She lifted her eyebrows at that. "Especially as a woman?"

"You know what I mean. I would never wish for you to change, but even the dragons who patrol Almack's are not as independent and impervious to scandal as you seem to be. It is like it does not even cross your mind that spending days in bed with a man might be scandalous."

"I did worry about your reputation," she muttered.

He snorted at that. "But not your own."

"No."

"So, tell me."

"Do you believe in magic?"

"Like witches?"

She nodded.

"I suppose," he said slowly.

"I didn't believe in magic until I arrived here. Just before you stopped our carriage, Alice said the most outlandish things and I thought she was lying, but she wasn't." He hadn't run out of the room yet, so she decided to keep going. "You see, I was living my sad little life and feeling rather pathetic about things when I saw a shop offering to arrange travel to other places."

"I hate hearing you don't like your life," Gray said, brushing his thumb over the back of her hand. "I would love to make you smile and laugh every day."

"Yes. Well." Her cheeks heated and she couldn't stop her smile. "That is when I met Alice. I didn't realize then, though, that Alice was a witch."

"A witch? I thought witches were just healers or wise women or..." He cast his gaze around the room as though searching for other descriptions. "I remember a rumor about a woman accused of being a witch a while ago, but in the end, it was her neighbors who were persecuted for attacking her. That was somewhere by Cambridge, if I remember correctly. But it was hardly the same as the witch trials from history. No one with sense believes accusations like that in today's world."

"I don't know about that woman, but witches exist. I know this because I am so far from home there is no other explanation but magic."

"Where is your home?"

She pulled the blanket tight around her shoulders. "This is going to sound unbelievable."

"Cassy," he urged, "just tell me."

"I come from..." She swallowed. Why was this so difficult? He took her hands in his. That small contact and seeing the way his hands cradled hers gave her the strength to keep talking. "I live in a city called Calgary. It is located in a province in the western part of Canada. And it's like two hundred years from now."

He blinked at her. "You mean you come from the future?"

"Yes. I know you probably think I'm insane now, but I swear to you it's the truth. The world is so different. That's why I act the way I do. I'm just an average woman where I come from. There is nothing particularly bold or outlandish or unique about me." She stared at their joined hands. "I don't want to leave you tomorrow, Gray. I don't want to be without you. But Alice left and I don't know how to do that magic. I don't even know how to get her to come back." She met his eyes then. "I don't even know if you would want to come with me."

"To the colonies?"

"Except it isn't a colony anymore. Not the way you're thinking about it. Canada is its own country and has been since 1867."

"1867." He said the year slowly like it was some mythical concept he couldn't even fathom. Would it be any different if someone had told her they'd come from 2062 or 2222? No way. She couldn't imagine what the world would look like then, although scenes from *The Jetsons* and *Star Trek* came to mind. Did Alice know? Could she go into the future as well as the past? Would Cassy even want to know what that future looked like?

"I know this is a lot to take in but, Gray, what if it were possible? What if you could come home with me?"

"To the future."

Cassy reached over and grabbed the ring from the table beside the bed. "Alice gave this to me before she left. Apparently, it has magic in it that can get me home."

Gray eyed the ring like he wanted to grab it, take it on a quest to Mordor, and throw it in the fires of Mount Doom. But he wouldn't understand the reference. He wasn't a hobbit, and Lord of the Rings hadn't been written yet.

"I will leave tomorrow with or without the ring," Cassy said as she pressed it into his palm. "Apparently that isn't up for debate. But Alice told me the ring can act independently of that. I think it could bring you to me. If that's what you would want. Or, you could just keep it, as a token of the time we've shared."

He closed his fingers around the ring and took a shaky breath. "I see now why you said all of this would sound fantastical, but, and I cannot believe I am going to say this, I believe you. What you have said resonates somehow. I do not understand it, but it is the same as the way I know we are meant to be together. I know you are telling me the truth."

"The ring is yours now," Cassy said. She stared at his hand holding the ring, before wrapping her hands around his. "Please. Keep it safe. I don't want you to answer me now, but I want you to keep this. If you decide you want to be with me, use this ring. Alice said you just need to be touching the ring and wish for home. But since you don't know anything about my home, maybe just think about me."

"You *are* my home," Gray whispered.

Tears welled in Cassy's eyes. "Don't make a rash decision. Just... just know you are always welcome. And maybe this ring could carry you to me. I don't know." She wiped at her eyes. "I'm going to find Alice when I get back. I'm going to see what I can do from my end too, okay? Because, Gray, I feel exactly the same way. You are my home too. And I really want you to court me. And I want us to smile and laugh every single day. I want to spend the rest of my life with you."

He pulled her into his arms. They clung to one another long into the night. Neither of them wanted to fall asleep, too scared they would wake up to find that everything had changed. Together they watched the morning light fall through the bedroom window. When a foreign tingling sensation tickled the back of her neck, she choked back a sob. As if sensing something was happening, Gray tightened his arms around her.

"I love you," she whispered.

And just before he disappeared from sight, she swore he said he loved her too.

CHAPTER 12

Magic always has the last say.
Grandma Lucy's Rules to Magic and Dating

Cassy was magically deposited inside her living room with all her luggage, her original clothing, and a shattered heart. Her legs gave way, and she sank to her sofa. Everything around her was familiar, from the shag carpet she'd been meaning to rip out for years to the stack of paperbacks on the side table by her sofa. The jigsaw puzzle she'd purchased on the winter solstice lay half-finished on her coffee table. That was how she'd expected to spend her holiday before she'd met Alice.

It didn't interest her in the least now.

Had she actually left? Had it just been a dream?

She grabbed her phone and looked at the date. December 31st. New Year's Eve. It was all there on the screen. She'd been gone for days.

What was Gray doing now? Was he thinking about using the ring? He had to believe her now, right? She'd disappeared right in front of him. She'd hoped he'd follow right behind her. He hadn't.

Maybe he decided he couldn't leave his life behind for a woman he'd known for less than a week. Or maybe it hadn't worked. She refused to look up his name on the internet. She refused to see if he married Charlotte. She refused to think of him as dead, even though he would have died two hundred years ago.

Cassy grabbed her keys and rushed to the door. She had to find Alice.

Twenty minutes later, she was standing outside the building where she'd first met the time traveling witch. The place was empty. Neglected. Nothing like what she remembered. She pressed her face against the grimy window. The sign for Gina's Time Travel Agency was nowhere to be seen. The dog and the cat? Not there. Alice? Again, not there. The inside looked like any other abandoned store with empty shelves, a pile of old hangers in the corner, and a desk against the far wall, nothing like it had looked when she'd been in there before Christmas.

She googled the business name and nothing remotely familiar appeared in the search results.

She cursed and felt more tears coming, but she didn't have time for that. If she'd found Alice once when she didn't even know magic existed, she could find her again now that she did know. Cassy closed her eyes and prodded her intuition.

"Come on, come on, come on..."

Nothing.

Her fledgling magic, if that's even what it was, was broken.

She visited the shops on either side of where the travel agency had been. No one knew Alice. That song by Smokie kept circling her thoughts. Who *was* Alice? Cassy wanted to know why she left and where she had to go.

After three hours of wandering up and down the street and every other street within a four-block radius, Cassy gave up. At least for the day. Her feet ached, she was hungry, and she needed a better plan. She was so tired at this point she couldn't think straight. She hadn't slept the night before and everything was catching up with her, all of it: the tension, the worry, and the unfulfilled wishes. All she wanted was to find a way to Gray and nothing was working the way she'd hoped it would.

When she arrived back home, the place was too quiet, not in the same way as the near silence of the cottage on a snowy morning, but in the echoing emptiness of a too lonely house. She ordered a pizza, started streaming *Pride and Prejudice* so the place wasn't quite so blah, and wished Gray were here with her.

Some New Year's Eve.

Just as Colin Firth was about to dive into the water, there was a loud explosive noise. It came from behind her house. Had someone crashed their car in the lane? She raced to the back door and wrenched it open in time to hear a burst of surprised masculine shouts.

Ignoring the cold, she ran barefoot into the snow. The air sparkled with what she now knew was magic around the one man she feared she'd never see again.

"Gray!" she shouted and threw herself at him. "You're here. You're really here."

"Cassy, Cassy, Cassy." He hugged her tightly and swung her around in a circle. "It worked. I cannot believe it. It actually worked. I tried to get here sooner, but I had to say goodbye to Reg and Lottie. For the longest time he refused to believe I was not simply drunk. I tried to get them to come too, but they wanted to stay. And then he helped me arrange my departure to look like I had been killed so the title could be passed along without fuss. Although, I think I managed to convince them to go to Gretna Green, just to be certain things go smoothly. And..." He stared into her eyes and seemed to forget his words. He smiled down at her with that same devilish grin that had entranced her from the first time they'd met. "I came as soon as I could."

"Can we save the happy reunions until we are somewhere warmer?" another man asked.

Gray laughed as he set her down. Then she discovered Duncan had come through time with Gray.

"Oh, wow," she said.

Duncan was vibrating with some strong emotion. Anger maybe? He looked ready to pounce. Instead, he marched up to her and stared down into her face. Power throbbed out from him in invisible waves. The threat in his stance was clear, but her intuition didn't say run, so she put her hands on her hips and stood her ground.

"Take a step back, Duncan," Gray said, pushing at Duncan's shoulder. The vampire didn't budge.

"Where is Alice?" Duncan demanded.

"I don't know. I've been looking for her all day."

His eyes glowed red as he scowled at her, but he finally stepped back. What did stress do to a vampire? Because he looked very stressed. She prayed he wouldn't attack anyone. She liked her blood inside her body, thank you very much.

"Let's go inside," Cassy said. "I'm freezing."

Then they both seemed to realize what she was wearing and gaped at her. The men were wearing the same clothes they would have in their own time, which made sense. Those clothes still existed now, although mostly just in museums or perhaps in the attics of really old houses. In contrast, she wasn't wearing anything remotely like a woman from their era. Her feet were bare. Her pajama bottoms had snowmen on them, and her top was an old threadbare T-shirt she kept for comfort instead of aesthetics. Her hair was probably a mess too, since she'd been burrowing in a blanket on her couch for hours as she watched Elizabeth and Darcy fall in love. Gray quickly took off his great coat and dropped it over her shoulders.

"Your feet," Gray said as he swept her up in his arms and carried her toward the door. "They must be frozen."

"Just like the first time we met, and you insisted I get out of the carriage in those silly shoes."

They filed into the house. She directed Gray to the living room, where he reluctantly let her down to stand on her own, and then she wasn't sure what to do. Yes, she'd invited Gray here, but she hadn't thought about the logistics. And now there was Duncan the vampire here too. They needed identification documents and jobs and...

She took a deep breath. She needed to slow down and take one thing at a time. Gray was here. Everything else could be figured out.

"Please come in. Find a place to sit." She worried her hands at their wide-eyed fascination with everything they saw. Gray was blinking uncomprehendingly at the movie playing on her TV. "Are you hungry? Thirsty?" She eyed Duncan. "I don't have any blood." She looked at the clock. This late on New Year's Eve, she doubted a butcher would be open. Would animal blood even work?

A sharp rap on her front door made her freeze. She definitely wasn't expecting anyone. And how would she explain having two strange men in period costume in her living room? A reenactment group? Method acting?

Knock. Knock. Knock. The pounding was getting louder, more insistent.

Whoever was at her door wasn't leaving.

"Stay here," she said to the men. Of course Gray ignored her and followed. The coat Gray had given her dragged over the floor as she made her way to the door.

An angry man with long teeth glared at them as he barged inside without saying a word. Behind him, a woman in a long flowing gown smiled serenely at them.

"Don't mind him," the woman said in an enchantingly musical voice as she followed the man inside. "He's always like this when he gets called out during the waxing moon. Just be happy it isn't a full moon tonight."

"I didn't call anyone."

"You didn't have to, my dear." The woman's laughter sounded like the most beautiful operatic solo. In fact, it was so beautiful it was eerily unsettling. Who were these people?

"I don't understand."

"It's magic," the woman said as she seemed to float over Cassy's awful shag carpet.

"Wolf," Duncan said. Oh boy. Were the vampire's teeth changing? Getting longer? That couldn't be a good thing. And, when he said wolf, did he mean werewolf?

"Duncan McAllister," the new man said in a faint Scottish brogue as he shook his head. "And here I thought you'd been staked and dusted centuries ago."

And then they were laughing and grabbing one another in an embrace. Did that mean this guy had been alive two hundred years ago? Wow. Yeah. She definitely needed to know more about this whole magic thing.

"Who are you?" Cassy pointed at the man and woman. "And what are you doing here?"

"I'm McKenna," the woman said. "An agent of the

Supernatural Society and lead siren in this area. And this is Fergus Coull. He is the werewolf designate. We have come because of a surge of unexpected magic in the area."

"Could smell it a mile away." Fergus rubbed his nose as if the scent was particularly unpleasant.

"Unauthorized time travel," McKenna said, shaking her head. "It always causes such a fuss."

"This is my fault," Cassy said quickly. She didn't want to get Alice in trouble. "I was given an object that could bring me home by my... time travel agent, I guess you'd call her. And I gave it to Gray. I couldn't leave him there. I just..." Her hands started to shake. "Please. You can't send him back."

Fergus rolled his eyes. "Fated mates. Always so dramatic."

McKenna patted Cassy's arm. "There, there, dear. We're just here to make sure everyone arrived safely and start the acclimation process."

"What do you mean by fated mates?" Gray asked.

"I can smell Fate's magic working to bind you together." The werewolf's nose twitched, and he looked ready to sneeze. "Congrats on the divine blessing and all that." He muttered those last words with a bored air that suggested they were common felicitations offered to new couples. Cassy had never heard the saying before, but it did sound like something Grandma Lucy would have said.

"So, everyone can stay?" Cassy had to make sure.

"Yeah, yeah," Fergus muttered. "Don't know why you had to do this tonight though. I had plans, you know? What with it being New Year's Eve and all."

"I do not need to acclimate," Duncan muttered as he turned toward the door. "I will find Alice."

"No, you won't. Not tonight," Fergus said.

When Duncan didn't stop, Fergus turned to McKenna. "Will you stop fang boy over there?"

Mackenna's lyrical voice filled the room. Everyone froze, but it was Duncan who truly appeared spellbound. He spun around and trudged back to the living room where he plopped down on her sofa. The song ended as abruptly as it had started. Duncan scowled and crossed his arms over his chest, but he didn't move toward the door again.

"And stay there," Fergus said. "I don't care if you are in another fated mate situation or any of that. You can wait until I say you can go. If you head out that door right now, you'll just bring the whole mundane world down on us." Fergus shook his head like Duncan was an idiot for even trying to leave. Then Fergus started muttering again as he pulled out a notebook from his jacket pocket.

Cassy didn't hear the rest of his complaints because Gray had captured her in his arms again.

"I love you, Cassy, with all my heart."

"I love you too, Gray. I don't know what I would have done if you hadn't come."

Then they were kissing as if they weren't in a room full of people.

"Ach, why are they kissing?" Fergus groaned.

MacKenna's melodic laughter rang through the air.

Honestly, though, Cassy didn't care what Fergus said. She couldn't imagine a more perfect way to ring in her New Year.

THE END

LET'S CONNECT

- Join Lori Whyte's newsletter here: loriwhye.com/newsletter (*This is the best way to find out about new releases and sales!*)
- Visit Lori's website at: loriwhyte.com
- Or follow Lori on:

  [f] facebook.com/LoriWhyteAuthor

  [BB] bookbub.com/authors/lori-whyte

LOTHIAN WEREWOLVES

A spin-off MF novel set in the same world as A Werewolf's Curse
A Wolf's Protection

MANNIX DRAGON SHIFTERS

MFM paranormal romances with hot dragons
Their Runaway Mate
Snowbound at Solstice (A Christmas Novella)
Mating of Convenience
Loving Her Dragons
Her Dragons, Her Mates (A Christmas Novella)
Mannix Dragon Shifters: The Complete Set

Find out more at loriwhyte.com